SUPERSTARS OF WRESTLING

BAYLEY

... PROUDFIT

Gareth Stevens

Please visit our website, www.garethstevens.com. For a free color catalog of all our high-quality books, call toll free 1-800-542-2595 or fax 1-877-542-2596.

Cataloging-in-Publication Data

Names: Proudfit, Benjamin.
Title: Bayley / Benjamin Proudfit.
Description: New York : Gareth Stevens Publishing, 2019. | Series: Superstars of wrestling | Includes index.
Identifiers: LCCN ISBN 9781538220931 (pbk.) | ISBN 9781538220917 (library bound) | ISBN 9781538220948 (6 pack)
Subjects: LCSH: Women wrestlers--United States--Biography--Juvenile literature. | Wrestlers--United States--Biography--Juvenile literature. | World Wrestling Entertainment, Inc.--Biography--Juvenile literature.
Classification: LCC GV1196.A1 P67 2019 | DDC 796.812092 B--dc23

First Edition

Published in 2019 by
Gareth Stevens Publishing
111 East 14th Street, Suite 349
New York, NY 10003

Designer: Sarah Liddell
Editor: Kristen Nelson

Photo credits: Cover, pp. 1, 11, 19 Lukas Schulze/Stringer/Bongarts/Getty Images; pp. 5, 29 PHILIPPE HUGUEN/Staff/AFP/Getty Images; p. 7 Tabercil/Wikimedia Commons; pp. 8, 15, 17 Wandering unicorn/Wikimedia Commons; p. 9 Walter McBride/Contributor/Corbis Entertainment/Getty Images; pp. 13, 23, 25 FlickrWarrior/Wikimedia Commons; p. 21 Prefall/Wikimedia Commons; p. 27 Orlando Sentinel/Contributor/Tribune News Service/Getty Images.

Printed in the United States of America

CPSIA compliance information: Batch #CS18GS: For further information contact Gareth Stevens, New York, New York at 1-800-542-2595.

CONTENTS

THE REAL DEAL

When fans of World Wrestling Entertainment (WWE) talk about Bayley, they say she's **genuine**, upbeat, and a true wrestling fan herself. Her character has made her a beloved part of the women's **division** of WWE!

IN THE RING

Bayley's fans love her willingness to high-five and hug them, living up to her T-shirt **slogans** like "I'm a Hugger!" and "Huggers Gonna Hug."

ON THE COURT

Bayley was born Pamela Rose Martinez on June 15, 1989, near San Jose, California. As a kid, Bayley played a lot of sports, including volleyball and track, but her main sport was basketball.

IN THE RING

Bayley was so good at basketball, she played on the **varsity** team all 4 years of high school. She was a team captain her senior year.

RING DREAMS

By the time Bayley was about 10, she was a huge wrestling fan. She watched it on TV every week. She also started going to live wrestling shows near San Jose. In school, Bayley wrote papers about her dream to be a wrestler!

RANDY SAVAGE

IN THE RING

Bayley has said her in-ring gear is based on the colorful, fun look of her favorite wrestler, "Macho Man" Randy Savage.

TRAINING BEGINS

When Bayley turned 18, she started training at a nearby wrestling school called Big Time Wrestling (BTW). She said when she started training in April 2008, the ropes bruised her ribs so badly "it hurt to be hugged."

IN THE RING

Bayley's first wrestling trainer told her to smile less! She says she was just having too much fun.

GOING PRO

Bayley had her first **professional** match just 5 months after she started training. She mostly wrestled for BTW for 4 years. In 2011, she **debuted** for SHIMMER, a women's-only wrestling company. Having matches in SHIMMER was a big goal of hers!

IN THE RING

When she wrestled for BTW and SHIMMER, Bayley was known as Davina Rose.

In December 2012, Bayley signed with WWE and started training for their NXT brand. In her first match in January 2013, she wore a mask! Then, she was given the name Bayley, a character she turned into a bubbly, spirited wrestling superfan.

IN THE RING

Sara Amato, a women's wrestler and trainer with WWE, said of Bayley: "She was such a hard worker, and it's not the easiest being a woman in this [business]. Bayley from the get-go stood out."

Bayley worked hard to get even better in the ring. She debuted on the *NXT* TV show a few months later in a singles match against NXT wrestler Paige. Soon after, Bayley started sporting her well-known side ponytail, hair bows, and headbands!

IN THE RING

Bayley became a leader in the locker room during her years at NXT. She said: "If the girls in NXT can remember things that they've learned from me that helped them, that just keeps building women's wrestling."

HUGGERS
GONNA
HUG

CHAMP CHANCES

In 2014, Bayley worked with the top women in NXT, including Sasha Banks, Alicia Fox, and AJ Lee. She finally got a championship match against Charlotte Flair in September 2014 at the special event, NXT TakeOver: Fatal 4-Way. She lost—but was ready for more chances!

CHARLOTTE FLAIR

Bayley, Charlotte Flair, Becky Lynch, and Sasha Banks were known as the Four Horsewomen when they were in NXT together.

Bayley's big moment came at NXT TakeOver: Brooklyn in August 2015. She took on NXT Women's Champion Sasha Banks in a match many called the best of the year. Some even called it the best women's match ever. And Bayley won!

IN THE RING

The other three Horsewomen were all called up to the main WWE **roster** in 2015, leaving Bayley behind in NXT.

SASHA BANKS

Sasha and Bayley had a rematch for the NXT Women's Championship at NXT TakeOver: Respect in October 2015. It was the first women's match to ever be the main event of an NXT special event! Bayley won, keeping the title.

IN THE RING

Bayley and Sasha's match made history as the first women's "Iron Man" match. In this kind of match, whoever gets the most **falls** in 30 minutes is the winner.

MOVING UP

In July 2016, Bayley appeared as Sasha Banks's surprise tag-team partner at the WWE **pay-per-view** (PPV) Battleground. However, she didn't officially join the main roster until the next month as part of the WWE TV show *Raw*.

ASUKA

IN THE RING

In 2016, Bayley had a number of great matches with Asuka in NXT. She eventually lost the NXT Women's Championship to Asuka at NXT TakeOver: Dallas.

During Bayley's first night on *Raw*, she challenged the Raw Women's Champion, Charlotte Flair, for her title. She didn't have the match that night, but Bayley would go on to beat Charlotte for the championship in February 2017.

IN THE RING

Bayley's win ended Charlotte's winning streak of 16 PPV wins in a row.

THE BIG RING

In April 2017, Bayley walked into WrestleMania 33 as the Raw Women's Champion. She won a Fatal 4-Way match against Charlotte Flair, Sasha Banks, and Nia Jax on the biggest wrestling stage of them all. Bayley's childhood dream came true!

ALEXA
BLISS

IN THE RING

Bayley lost the Raw Women's Championship to Alexa Bliss soon after WrestleMania—but she's working to get it back!

THE BEST OF BAYLEY

SIGNATURE MOVES
suplex, diving back elbow, hurricanrana

FINISHERS
Bayley-to-belly suplex

ACCOMPLISHMENTS
NXT Women's Champion, WWE Raw Women's Champion, took part in the first women's Iron Man match against Sasha Banks

MATCH TO WATCH
NXT TakeOver: Brooklyn vs. Sasha Banks

FOR MORE INFORMATION

BOOKS

Kortemeier, Todd. *Superstars of WWE*. Mankato, MN: Amicus High Interest, 2017.

Pantaleo, Steve. *How to Be a WWE Superstar*. New York, NY: DK Publishing, 2017.

WEBSITES

Bayley
www.wwe.com/superstars/bayley
Keep up-to-date with Bayley in WWE here!

BayleyFansite.com
bayleyfansite.com
Check out a fan's website dedicated to Bayley!

GLOSSARY

debut: to appear for the first time

division: a group of people within a bigger company

fall: a pin, or a way of winning a wrestling match in which one wrestler holds the other's shoulders on the mat for a certain amount of time, commonly 3 seconds in WWE

genuine: true, real

pay-per-view (PPV): an event that can only be seen on a TV channel if viewers pay a fee

professional: earning money from an activity that many people do for fun

roster: the list of people who are on a team

slogan: a word or group of words that's easy to remember

varsity: the main sports team of a school

INDEX